TOO CLOSE FOR COMFORT

A TABOO ROMANCE

VICTORIA RUSH

VOLUME 36

JADE'S EROTIC ADVENTURES - BOOK 36

COPYRIGHT

For the uninhibited...

WANT TO AMP UP YOUR SEX LIFE?

Sign up for my newsletter to receive more free books and other steamy stuff. Discover a hundred different ways to wet your whistle!

Victoria Rush Erotica

1

———

As I watched our 787 Dreamliner arc over Biscayne Bay on approach to Miami International Airport, I couldn't help thinking back on fond memories from my youth. My brother Stephen and I had grown up on the northern shores of Chicago, where we made frequent trips to the beaches of Lake Michigan with our parents, frolicking in the surf and playing with our water toys until the sun went down.

But it had been almost five years since I'd seen Stephen after he took an executive position with American Airlines and married his college sweetheart, Gabriella. We'd tried to stay in touch as best we could from afar, but our communications seemed to be more and more focused on his struggling career with the airline. His job as Vice-President of Marketing had become increasingly strained in the midst of continual downsizing and consolidation in the industry following the last big recession.

In addition to the never-ending pressure to boost revenues in the super-competitive business, he'd grown fearful of the constant layoffs, worried when his own job might be on the cutting block. I'd hoped by visiting him that I could take his mind off work for a little while and reflect on happier times. Plus, I hadn't seen Gabby since their wedding ceremony on the North Shore, and I was looking forward to getting caught up with both of them.

As the jet's altitude lowered approaching the city, I could see the trails of motorboats and jet-skis plying the turquoise waters off Miami Beach. Little parasols dotted the beach as people lounged on the sand, periodically wading into the frothy waves. It had been far too long since I'd experienced the sublime sensation of warm saltwater rolling over my bare feet, and I could feel my skin tingling at the thought of finding some quality downtime with Gabby and Steve.

When the plane skidded down onto the runway, I turned on my phone and sent a message to Steve to let him know I'd arrived. He'd promised to pick me up at the airport and drive me back to his home in Coral Gables. After I picked up my luggage at the baggage claim carousel and headed toward the ground transportation area of the terminal, I saw him waiting near the exit door, and he waved at me. He looked weary and pale, but he still had that thick shock of curly blond hair I remembered as a kid and the handsome smile that had convinced his pretty bride to move halfway across the country in pursuit of his new job.

When we greeted, he gave me a big hug and kissed me on the cheek.

"How was the flight?" he said. "Did you enjoy the first-class seats I arranged for you through the Friends and Family Program?"

"Yes," I said. "But it was hardly necessary for such a short flight. Though I did enjoy the view from my window seat on the right-hand side of the plane. The beaches look spectacular along the east side. I'm looking forward to getting out in the sun again after a long winter."

I took a moment to appraise his pallid complexion and two-day-old growth of beard.

"It looks like you could use a bit of sunshine and fresh air yourself. You're looking far too pale for someone who lives right next to one of the most popular tourist destinations in America."

"Humpf," Stephen grunted. "If only I could find the time away from work. With all the pressures and downsizing in the airline industry over the past few years, it's been all-hands-on-deck just trying to stay afloat. If I don't put in the extra hours, I'm afraid my job will be the next one to be made redundant."

"Let's not worry about any of that right now," I smiled. "Let's just pretend like we're eight years old again and lap up this little slice of paradise for the next week or so."

I looked around the terminal for any sign of his wife.

"Where's Gabby? I've been looking forward to seeing her almost as much as you. We never really got a chance to become properly acquainted after you moved to Florida."

"She wanted to prepare a nice homecoming meal for the three of us. Plus, traffic at this time of day is pretty crazy. It's not much fun navigating the smog-choked streets of Miami during rush hour."

"Okay, Mr. Sourpants," I chuckled. "I feel really sorry for you, with your glamorous job and cushy lifestyle in this little patch of Eden.

"Come on," I said, threading my arm between his, and pulling my roller bag toward the exit. "Let's get out of this busy terminal and go see your pretty wife."

———

On the drive back to his place, I tried to take Stephen's mind off his troubles by talking about the old days and laughing about all the shenanigans we got into as kids, but I could tell that his mind was elsewhere as he asked me half-heartedly about what was going on in my life. When we turned into the gated neighborhood of Gables Estates and drove up his long brick-lined driveway toward his pink stucco house, I gasped.

"Holy crap, Steve!" I gushed. "You're really moving up in the world!"

"Hardly," he huffed. "This is just a middle-class property in this part of Miami. The *real* money is out on the islands and in Palm Beach. You should *see* some of the estates along the shoreline."

"I wouldn't sell yourself short," I said, admiring the manicured gardens surrounding his house with tall hibiscus trees and brightly colored flowers. "It looks to me like you're doing pretty well for yourself."

"Come," he said, parking his Audi in the driveway. "You must be hungry after traveling half the day. Gabby's eager to see you again."

He led me into the house, where I admired his marble floors and upscale Miami decor. With tall ceilings and huge picture windows overlooking a large garden, his home looked like the epitome of laid-back southern lifestyle. But when I saw Gabby working in the large open kitchen, my attention was suddenly diverted to the more natural features of the home. Wearing a tight-fitting apron around her curvy figure with her hair tied up in a bun atop her head, she looked even more beautiful than I remembered her at their wedding.

"Jade!" she exclaimed when she caught sight of me entering the room. "It's seems like forever since I last saw you!"

She dropped her cooking utensils and rushed toward me, throwing her arms around my back. I could feel her firm breasts pressing against me, and I blushed self-consciously at the visceral reaction to her touch.

"I know," I sighed. "Five years is way too long for close family not to see one another. I've been looking forward to this trip for ages."

I glanced at Gabby's pretty cooking uniform and nodded approvingly.

"I see the passage of time has been good to you. You look even more gorgeous than ever, as if that were even possible."

"I was just about to say the same thing about you," she said. "I love that new bob hairstyle."

She glanced down my body, running her eyes up and down my figure.

"And what have you been doing to stay in shape? You look as buff as always. It can't just be *yoga* that's giving you all those beautiful curves?"

"I've been getting my exercise in *lots* of novel ways," I smiled, not quite ready to tell her and Stephen about my recent forays into the arms of lesbian lovers.

"Well whatever you're doing, you'll have to share your secret with me. This southern lifestyle can be a little too laid-back sometimes to keep up my girly figure."

"Um, I think you're managing just fine in spite of the unfortunate surroundings you find yourself in," I said, peering sarcastically around their luxurious house.

"Okay, enough self-congratulations, you two lovebirds," Stephen interjected. "I'm starved. What's that exquisite concoction I'm smelling on the stove?"

"I made one of your favorite meals in honor of your sister's arrival," Gabby said. "Ventresca tuna with whole wheat pasta and kalamata olives in homemade tomato sauce. It's just about ready." Gabby handed me a bottle of wine and pointed toward the preset table. "Do you want to pour the wine, Jade? This Malbec goes perfect with tuna."

"My pleasure," I smiled. "I could do with a couple of glasses of wine to decompress after a day of traveling."

<hr>

The three of us got caught up over dinner, and I was happy to see Stephen relaxing a bit while we all laughed about our childhoods and talked about current developments. Steve and Gabby made occasional intimations about developments in my love life after my marriage had quickly dissolved, but I told them I was taking my time exploring the dating field once again.

But I couldn't help noticing a certain emotional distance between the two of them. They hardly looked at each other the entire time during the meal and their chairs at the table seemed unnaturally far apart for a married couple. At first, I chocked it up to the size of their large dining room table, but when Stephen excused himself after an hour or so to get caught up on some overdue work in his study, I couldn't help probing a little further with Gabby while we cleaned up in the kitchen.

"How's everything been going down here in la-la land?" I said, drying off the pots and pans as she placed them in the opposite side of the sink after washing them. "Stephen seems a little more distracted than usual."

Gabby paused for a moment while she nodded toward the suds in the basin.

"He hasn't been quite the same since he took that executive position at the airline. At first, I attributed it up to his desire to get ahead and consolidate his position at the firm. But with all the layoffs and competitive pressures the past few years in the industry, I think he's grown increasingly worried about keeping his job. We're carrying a pretty big mortgage, and he's always been mindful of his role as the primary breadwinner in the family."

"Hmm," I nodded sympathetically. "I can see how that might weigh on his mind. And what about the two of you? Have you been thinking about expanding the family with the pitter-patter of little feet in this marble palace of yours?"

"*God*, no," she frowned. "Now is definitely not the right time. We'd need two fully participating parents to make that work. Besides, it takes a certain degree of physical intimacy to make babies these days. Stephen's been so self-absorbed in his work the past few months, he barely touches me anymore. I can't even remember the last time we had sex."

"Wow," I said. "I'm sorry to hear that. A healthy sex life is an important part of a successful marriage. Maybe we can take his mind off work for a few days while I'm down here visiting. Go down to the beach and frolic in the surf, and all that. Maybe if he sees you in skimpy bikini again, it'll change his mind about attending to your female needs."

"I'd like that," Gabby said, putting the clean pots back into the kitchen cupboard. "But I might need to update my swimsuit if I hope to arouse his passions again. All I've got left in my wardrobe is a frumpy old one-piece suit from back in the day."

I took a quick look at her generous bosom bulging out from the top of her apron and shook my head.

"Well we can't have that Goddess figure of yours all covered up in nylon while we're strutting along South

Beach. What do you say the two of us go shopping tomorrow to pick out the perfect temptation? I could use a bit of a refresh to my summer wardrobe too!"

2

———

Gabby and I stayed up late after washing the dishes and finished a couple more bottles of wine while chatting about what each of us had been up to in the intervening years. She seemed to be particularly interested in my love life, and after my third glass of wine, I finally confessed about my recent excursions into the realm of lesbian and bisexual sex.

She wanted to know all the dirt on my lovers, with explicit details about the different ways we made love. I could tell she was intrigued, having never experimented outside her monogamous relationship with Stephen, and I found myself becoming increasingly turned on sharing the sordid details of my adventurous new sex life. I noticed her squirming on the sofa while I explained how sex with other women had been so much more fulfilling than the boring, straight sex I'd had with my previous husband.

By the time we retired to our separate bedrooms at three in the morning, I was wet as a leaky faucet and had to relieve my sexual tension by masturbating quietly under the covers. I wondered if she was doing the same thing, and even though I felt guilty about telling my sister-in-law about the pleasures of lesbian love, I figured rekindling her interest in sex in any way could only be good for their moribund marriage.

With the next day falling on a Saturday, after much cajoling and prodding, we finally convinced Stephen to join the two of us for a relaxing day at the beach. Hoping to surprise him with Gabby's sexy new swimsuit, we agreed to meet on the surf side of the Royal Palm Hotel at two in the afternoon. That would give Gabby and me enough time to do a little shopping and develop a plan of attack for enticing him back under the covers with his wife.

Gabby took me to Miami's premiere shopping mall at Bal Harbour, and we flitted from one designer boutique to another before deciding that the Saks Fifth Avenue store had the best selection of swimsuits. We shared a small dressing room where we both tried on different outfits, giggling and baring our bodies while changing clothes. Gabby had a magnificent figure with tall, prominent, scooped-shaped breasts and slender hips that reminded me of a young Gina Lollobrigida. It was hard for me to concentrate while she asked my opinion about the different outfits she tried on while swaying her hips and mouth-watering tits mere inches away from my body in the small enclosed space.

As we changed from one outfit to another, she grew increasingly brazen and forward with her the comments about my revealing bikinis. After forty-five minutes or so of increasing sexual tension in the room, we accidentally bumped our hips together while bending over to remove another outfit, then swung around and straightened up, slapping our bare breasts against one another. We both paused momentarily, surprised at the unexpected touching of our private parts, then we suddenly melded together, embracing each other in a passionate kiss and intertwining of arms and legs.

Within seconds, our hands were running wildly over each other's bodies, dipping into every crevasse and squeezing each other's flesh with reckless abandon. Gabby seemed a little unsure how to engage with me as she groped me awkwardly while rubbing her crotch against mine, trying to increase the friction between our pussies. I lifted her left leg and bent her knee to the side, then raised my opposite knee, pinning her against the wall. When she felt my hot sex press against her own, she gasped, throwing her head back.

Not wanting to make too much commotion in the public dressing room, I pressed my mouth harder against her lips to stifle her moans while I ran my fingers through her hair and ground my wet pussy against hers. I could feel rivers of lubrication running down the insides of my legs, not sure if it was her or me that was getting more turned on by our clandestine public tryst. Deep down, I knew that it was wrong of me to take advantage of her vulnerability, especially in view of her fragile relationship with my brother, but there was something about her innocent inexperience and radiant beauty that I found simply irresistible.

As we rolled our sweaty bodies together and humped our hips together against the flimsy dividing wall of our small room, I could hear the creaking of the framework giving way to our impassioned fucking. Gabby's squeals and whimpering were growing louder and more prominent in spite of my best attempts to keep her vocalizations in check with my tongue in her mouth, but by this time I no longer cared who or how many people could hear us.

I could feel my own orgasm beginning to well up inside

me, and from the increasingly tight grip of Gabby's hands on my butt cheeks, I knew it wouldn't be long before her passion crested along with mine. As my climax washed over me, I lifted Gabby's body up in the air, pounding my wet cunt against hers and burying my face in her cleavage as I began to gush like a geyser all over her ass and the dressing room wall. When Gabby felt me squirting on her pussy, her eyes flung open in surprise and she threw her head back against the wall, grunting loudly in the throes of a powerful orgasm.

We held each other tightly while we moaned together in mutual climax, jerking our hips loudly against the thin partition in tandem with our powerful internal contractions. When we finally came down from our intense orgasm, I gently lowered her back down onto the floor as we panted heavily, leaning exhausted against the dressing room wall. After a few moments, we pulled back a few inches and peered into each other's faces.

"Holy shit!" Gabby panted. "*Now* I see why you were so interested in switching sides. That might have been the best sex I've had in my entire life!"

"You were probably just overly excited from all the pent-up frustration of not having had sex with your husband for such a long time. I don't want you to get any crazy ideas. You're still a married woman, you know. To my *brother*, no less."

"We can't ever *tell* him about this," she said, shaking her head as the reality of what we'd just done took hold of her.

"Of course not," I said. "This will be our little secret. What happens in Saks, stays in Saks."

"Ha," Gabby chuckled nervously. "What now? Do you think anybody heard us?"

"I don't see how they couldn't have *not* heard us. You

were pretty vocal, and this flimsy wall was shaking the whole time like a snare drum in a seventies pop band."

"Not to mention all the *mess* we've made of this place," she said, noticing the wet stain I'd left on the wall behind her. "I had no idea girls could squirt like that when they had sex."

"You've got a lot to learn, little lady," I grinned. "It's kind of an acquired skill. But I've always been a little wetter than most girls when I have good sex. And that was pretty fucking spectacular."

"Maybe you can teach me how to do that some day," Gabby said, smiling back at me mischievously. "I'm pretty sure if I pulled that little trick out of the hat while I was in bed with Stephen, that would bring some life back into his limp noodle."

I nodded as my pussy twitched watching her still-erect nipples jutting out from her plump breasts.

"We'll see what we can do to find some more private time while I'm in town. But we'll have to be careful that Stephen doesn't find out. I'm sure he wouldn't look kindly upon his long-lost sister taking advantage of his neglected wife while he's hosting me at your house."

I peered at the wet mark left from my spray on the wall as it dribbled down the sideboard.

"Let's clean up and get out of here before they send security to cart us away. Have you decided on a favorite outfit?"

"I was thinking of the cross-hatch-top and high-cut-bottom design in the hot pink color. I like how it supports my boobs and exposes just enough of my butt to highlight my best assets."

"I totally agree," I nodded.

I pulled some wet-wipes out of my purse that I kept on hand for these types of contingencies, then I wiped down the wall and we both got dressed and exited the dressing room area under the watchful gaze of many shellshocked surrounding shoppers. As we paraded down the hall hand-in-hand with everybody's eyes following us, the Saks dressing room attendant smiled and winked at us as we headed to the nearest cash register to pay for our purchases.

A few hours later, we met Stephen at the edge of the shoreline a few hundred feet opposite the hotel, just as Gabby was emerging from the surf with her wet bikini clinging to her luscious figure like a second skin. Stephen peered at her with wide eyes, appraising her from head to foot as he slowly lowered his sunglasses over his nose.

"Glad you could make it," I said, leading him up to our little stand on the beach a few feet way. "I was afraid you might get caught up in your work again and miss this opportunity to catch some fresh air and sunshine."

"How could I turn down an opportunity to mingle with my two favorite girls on such a pretty day?" he said, his eyes still darting over Gabby's sexy figure.

"Hi honey," Gabby said, giving him a peck on the cheek with wet lips as she traipsed up the sand toward us. "Do you like my new outfit?"

"Um—yes," Stephen stammered. "It's quite...*revealing*."

"Oh?" Gabby said, tilting her backside up teasingly to peer at her half-covered ass. "Do you think too much?"

"No..." Stephen said, noticing a parade of buff young men in Speedos checking out his wife as they passed by. "I'm just worried about you attracting the attention of all the *other* men on this beach in that hot outfit."

"I wouldn't worry about any of them," she smiled. "You

know I've only got eyes for you. Besides, what about Jade? Don't you think she looks just as sexy in her new outfit?"

"Well–yes," Stephen said, taking a cursory glance at my bikini. "But she's my *sister*, so I wouldn't say she's sexy so much as beautiful. You both look gorgeous as a matter of fact. You guys can definitely hold your own with all these preening teenagers and trophy wives strutting their wares on this beach."

"Well come on, then," I said, grabbing his hand. He looked slim and fit in his tight-fitting boxer-brief swim trunks, but definitely like he hadn't seen any sunshine for a long time. "Let's get that chiseled body of yours all tanned up so you don't stick out like a tourist among all these beautiful people."

Gabby and I grabbed each of his hands and pulled him toward the surf, where he crashed into an incoming wave with the water spraying all over the three of us.

That won't be the only thing spraying over him pretty soon with any luck, I smiled, watching the salty froth running down over Gabby's exposed belly and low-cut bikini.

3

Gabby, Stephen, and I stayed on the beach for a couple of hours before returning later in the day to the hotel for a long dinner and nightcap. I tried to convince Steve to join Gabby and me nightclub hopping along the strip, but he said his sunburn was bothering him, and he insisted on going home to catch up on work email. Not wanting to miss a chance to have more quality time with Gabby, the two of us danced well into the night, bumping and grinding our bodies together on the dance floor, getting more than a little tipsy in the process.

By the end of the evening, we were belting out our favorite pop songs on the taxi ride home while making out in the back seat. I was disappointed when we had to retire to our separate chambers, but neither one of us wanted to raise any suspicion on Stephen's part by having her join me in my bedroom. I had hoped that after seeing her in her sexy new swimsuit and enjoying some downtime away from the distractions of work that it might renew his sexual interest in Gabby. But not long after she closed the door, I was surprised to hear an argument emanating from their quarters instead of the sounds of lovemaking.

After a half hour or so of raised voices, it became quiet again in the house, and I lay awake tossing and turning while reliving the exciting encounter with Gabby in the dressing room at Saks. As much as I'd enjoyed our risky public tryst, I longed to lie down with her in the comfort of my own bed and make love to her slowly and properly. As I began to thread my fingers between my legs to relieve the growing ache in my pussy, I heard my door squeak open and I saw Gabby tiptoeing toward my bed.

"Do you mind if I join you for a little while?" she whispered in the dark.

"Of course not," I said, flipping back the covers. "I was just thinking about you too."

"I couldn't sleep," Gabby said, sliding her naked body in next to me. "I can't stop thinking about what we did in the dressing room earlier today."

"Me too," I said, snuggling closer to her. "But what was all that fighting I heard coming from your bedroom? After seeing Stephen eyeing you up at the beach, I was sure he'd be all over you as soon as you got home."

"It was something he said while we were out earlier in the day that bothered me," she said, looking at me with a pained expression. "That comment about all the pretty teenage girls and trophy wives showing off their wares on the beach. It made me feel old and cheap. I told him that he shouldn't be comparing me to anyone else, and that he should be damn happy to have snared a catch like me. Not many wives would put up with his constant bellyaching and long hours at work."

"I'm sorry to hear that," I said, wrapping my arms around her shoulders. "You're damn right that he should consider himself lucky to have landed you as his bride. You're a million times sexier than any of those silicone-enhanced bimbos, and you're an absolute *angel* to have put up with his neglect these past few years."

I ran my index finger slowly down the hollow of her spine toward the curvature of her tight ass.

"But I'm kind of glad that you came to me for consolation. I haven't been able to sleep either thinking about our encounter in the dressing room, and I was just about to relieve myself when you came in."

"Maybe I can help you with that," Gabby said, nibbling me softly on my neck.

"I was hoping you'd feel that way," I smiled, curving my hand around her back to caress the side of her breast. "But we're going to have to be quiet as mice this time. We can't make the same kind of commotion we did at Saks. Stephen would never forgive either one of us if he found us in bed together."

"I promise to be quiet this time," she said, wrapping her legs around my hips and pulling our crotches closer together. "Can you teach me how to squirt like you do? I want to come all over you like you did with me."

"Maybe we should take it slow, to start," I said. "As eager as I am to feel you squirting all over me, I'm not sure I can trust you to keep quiet under the circumstances. We've got all week to get to know each other a little better. I just want to be close to you right now. I feel like making love to you this time, instead of just *fucking* each other."

"I like the sound tof that," Gabby said. "I've been having the same kinds of feelings about you. In fact, I haven't felt this way in a long time."

"You mean sexually?"

"No, I mean emotionally. It's been nice to feel a two-way

connection again. And I have to confess, I've always had a bit of a crush on you. I was disappointed when Stephen moved us away from Chicago–"

"Oh Gab," I sighed, pulling her closer. "Maybe this isn't such a good idea after all. I don't want to drive a wedge between the two of you..."

"There's not much more distance you could possibly put between us right now," she said. "He's so self-absorbed in his work, even that sexy bikini I wore today couldn't do anything to perk up his interest in me."

"But what about *us*?" I said, peering into her pretty brown eyes. "I'm going to have to leave in a few days. This will just make it harder for us to separate–"

"Let's not worry about any of that right now," she said, rolling on her side to squeeze our bodies together. "We could never stay together permanently, anyhow. The rest of your family would never forgive us, and it would forever ruin your relationship with your brother. Let's just live in the moment and enjoy the brief time we have together while we can."

"You're twisting my arm, girl," I smiled, nibbling on one of her ears.

"Mmm," Gabby purred. "I like the feel of your tongue on my skin. I've been dreaming about you licking me all over. You have no idea how much I've fantasized about making love to you ever since we met at Stephen's dorm party all those years ago."

"Well just lie back and enjoy it then," I said, shifting my body lower on her body.

As Gabby lay trembling on the bedsheets with her arms lying expectantly by her side, I nibbled my way down the side of her neck and over the curvature of her shoulder, swiping my cheeks softly against the upper surface of her breasts.

"God, Jade," she moaned. "You really know how to drive a girl crazy. Stephen only seems interested in one part of me, and he's always in a hurry to get there to finish his business."

"We'll have to work on that," I said. "Perhaps you can teach him some of these new techniques. Sometimes I think only a *woman* knows how to properly please another woman."

"Yes," Gabby sighed. "Teach me all the ways of making love to a woman. I want to feel every part of you touching my body. Your skin feels so soft against mine."

"Mmm," I purred as I buried my face in her cleavage, then lifted my head to let the ends of my curls dance over her erect nipples.

"*Huh!*" Gabby suddenly gasped at the pleasant sensation on her sensitive skin. "Damn–I could make love to you every night this way."

"I don't know about *every* night," I said, lowering my lips to kiss her protruding tips. "How sound a sleeper is Stephen?"

"Can't you hear him snoring in the other room?"

I stopped shifting under the covers for a moment and smiled when I heard the familiar wheezing of a man's voice deep in slumber coming from the room down the hall.

"Good," I said. "Maybe that'll help cover up all the noise you make when you make love. Should I get you something to clamp your teeth onto to keep you from waking up the whole house?"

"In due time," Gabby purred. "I'm pretty sure I can find something tasty to chomp on when you're finished down there."

"I'll be happy to oblige," I smiled. "Just pull the covers

over your head in the meantime if you need to muffle your moans. Because by the time I'm finished with you, I intend to have you squealing like a pig."

Gabby scrunched further down under the covers and pulled the sheets over her head, then she spread her legs apart, inviting me to go lower. I could feel her nipples tickling my breasts, and unable to resist the temptation any further, I devoured them like a newborn calf sucking on its mother's teat for the first time. She arched her back when she felt my mouth encircle her medallions, groaning softly under the covers. Her tits were soft but firm, and I squeezed them gently while I suckled on her peaks.

I was surprised how big they felt in my mouth, almost the size of a young boy's penis. I circled my tongue around the phallic projection, slipping it in and out of my mouth, making a rude popping sound each time. She groaned each time I did so, and the harder I sucked on it, the bigger it seemed to grow. Not wanting to neglect her other breast, I switched back and forth between each of her tips, teasing and bending them in my mouth.

I could feel her hips gyrating more vigorously against my tummy while I was sucking her, and after five minutes or so of playing with her tits, I drew my tongue down the crease in the center of her stomach toward her quivering pussy. When I reached her pubis, I was surprised at how soft and bare it was, and I peered up at her for a moment.

"You're awfully well-groomed for someone who hasn't had sex in such a long time," I smiled. "Have you been expecting some new attention down here lately?"

"I wanted to make sure I was properly landscaped to show off my low-cut bikini," she said. "But I decided to shave it all off knowing there was a good chance you'd see me naked in the change room."

"Well I *like* it," I purred, sucking her bare flesh hard into my mouth.

"Yes, Jade," Gabby panted. "Suck my pussy. I want you to taste me *everywhere*."

"Mmm, my pleasure," I said, lowering my chin down into her dripping crease.

I could feel the heat from her pussy radiating against my face and neck, and I spread her knees further apart, kissing the insides of her thighs as I slowly worked my way up to her steamy opening. Gabby whimpered as she tilted her hips toward me, begging me to approach her prize, but I wanted to build the tension to make her first experience with lesbian oral sex as memorable as possible. But when I felt her juices beginning to pour down over her thighs and I tasted her aroma on my tongue, I positioned my head over her puffy lips and sucked them into my mouth with a loud sopping sound.

"*Uhnn!*" Gabby grunted, reaching down under the covers to grab the back of my head and pull me harder into her pussy.

She was gyrating her hips harder and faster now that I'd made contact with her most sensitive parts, and the bed started to creak and shake in tandem with her escalating moans.

"You're going to have to be quieter if we're going to do this without waking your husband up," I said, pausing momentarily to chide her. "Stop rocking the bed so much!"

"Sorry," she said, lifting the covers to peer down at me. "But you're making it nearly impossible for me to remain still when you do that to me. I've never had anybody turn me on this much!"

"Do you want me to *stop*?" I teased.

"Don't you dare!" she hissed. "I promise to be quieter. Just suck my pussy a little longer. It won't take long for me to come soon."

"Okay," I said. "But I'll to have to stop if you can't control yourself any better. The last thing we need is for Stephen to barge in here and find his sister eating out his wife's pussy."

"Yes—eat my pussy, Jade," Gabby groaned. "Make me come in your mouth. I'm so wet right now, I feel like I'm about to spray all over you like a *car wash!*"

"Okay, just let your *pussy* do the talking the rest of the way. I'll know we're finished when I feel you cumming all over my face."

"Suck my clit now," she said. "I'm ready to come for you."

As much as I wanted to tease her a little longer, I was mindful of Stephen sleeping only a few feet down the hall, and we needed to get this over with before he suspected any foul play. I shifted my body a few inches higher between her legs, then slowly lowered my face over her folds, taking her engorged button into my mouth.

"Mmmft!" Gabby grunted, gritting her teeth trying to stifle her moans.

I could feel her gripping the sheets beside me with her two fists as she pressed her pussy harder against my face. I slid both of my hands under her ass and grabbed her butt cheeks, squeezing them hard as my tongue circled her nub, sucking it harder into my mouth as she slowly lifted her hips off the mattress. Her breathing began escalating rapidly in both pitch and frequency, and with her hips now raised almost two feet over the mattress and her buttock muscles tensing tightly in my hands, she suddenly let out loud squeal, and I felt her gushing into my mouth.

I threw one of my hands up toward her face, clamping it tightly over her mouth trying to muffle the sounds of her powerful climax, and I could hear Stephen's snoring temporarily interrupted while Gabby whimpered and moaned in tortured silence as her hips buckled against my face and her juices poured down over my chin. For almost a full minute, she stayed in this arched position, jerking her hips spastically against my face as jet after jet of her sweet cum filled my mouth.

When I felt her begin to climax, I stopped moving my tongue over her clit and just held her tightly, feeling her pussy clamping in rhythmic contractions against my face until she lowered her hips back down onto the bed and exhaled in one long, heavy sigh.

"Oh my *God!*" she whispered to me under the covers. "That was *insane!* I've never had an orgasm like that. Did you feel me come?"

"I felt you, I tasted you, and heard you," I said, nestling up beside her and holding her gently in my arms. "I just hope we haven't woken up your husband with all the noise you were making."

We both paused for a long moment to listen for any sound coming from the other room, and after a minute or so, the sound of Stephen's snoring began to fill the hallway again between our two rooms.

"Thank God," Gabby sighed when she realized he'd fallen back into a deep sleep. "Now I can return the favor and give you the same kind of pleasure you just gave me."

"As much as I like that idea," I said, caressing her soft hair. "I thinking we're pushing our luck as it is. Let me just hold you in my arms and enjoy your afterglow while he's still asleep. Maybe we can steal some more time together another night. That orgasm of yours was strong enough to satisfy *both* of us."

"Did I do good?" Gabby whispered, raising her eyebrows expectantly at me. "Did I squirt when I came?"

"Yes," I smiled. "Can't you see the wetness all over my face and breasts?"

"Mmm, yes," Gabby mewed, leaning over to kiss me passionately on my lips. "Tomorrow night I'm going to taste *your* pussy in my mouth and enjoy a little car wash of my *own*."

4

G abby and I fell asleep together not long after and were awoken a few hours later by a gentle tap on my bedroom door.

"Hello?" Stephen's voice called. "Has anyone seen any sign of my wife?"

Gabby woke up with a start and looked at me with wide eyes, unsure how to handle the awkward situation.

"It's okay," I whispered. "Get up quietly and put on a pair of pj's from my suitcase lying on the chair."

She scampered out of bed and found my pajamas in the case, hopping from one foot to the other while hastily pulling them over her naked body.

"I dunno," I called back to Stephen teasingly. "Have you checked the kitchen?"

"Yes," he said, sounding annoyed. "There's no sign of her anywhere in the house."

"What about the *laundry* room?" I said, getting up to put on some panties and a long button-up blouse.

"Nooo," Stephen groaned, beginning to catch on to my joke.

"Have you tried the garden?" I said, motioning for Gabby to get back into the bed and sit up against the headboard. "She must be *somewhere* around the place doing her wifely duties."

"Ha, ha–very funny," he said as I hopped back into the bed, sitting up beside Gabby with my legs crossed casually in front of me.

"Why don't you come in here and check under the bed? Are you sure you didn't scare her away last night with all your yelling?"

The door creaked open a bit and Stephen poked his head in, noticing us both sitting up nonchalantly in my bed like we'd been up chatting all night.

"*There* you are," he said, noticing Gabby peering back at him icily. "I was worried when I saw the car in the driveway and couldn't find you anywhere."

"I'm surprised you even noticed my absence, with your preoccupation with so many *other* things these days," she said, crossing her arms over her chest. "Maybe if you had a proper *trophy* wife, she'd be a little more doting of your every little whim and need–"

"Gabby," Stephen said, putting on his best puppy dog face. "I'm so sorry I said that. I didn't mean to compare you to anybody. You're the best trophy–I mean *wife*–any man could hope to have. I'm the luckiest man alive to have you put up with all my bullshit."

"Damn right," Gabby said, crossing her legs in front of her in solidarity with me.

"You guys look like two little bees in a bonnet," Stephen said, appraising our unusual sleepwear. "Have you been here all night?"

"Pretty much," I nodded. "You know how us girls like to sleep together and talk all night long. Plus, we got a little tipsy at the nightclub and crashed not long after we got home."

"Hmm," Stephen nodded, glancing at my bare legs suspiciously.

"Are you guys hungry? I was going to scare up an omelette if you're interested."

"I could practically eat a horse after dancing all night long. What about you, Gab?"

"I need to eat *something*, that's for sure," she said. "Are you sure you can manage it all by yourself, dear? Do you need me to crack the eggs for you or show you how to turn on the stove?"

"Very funny," Stephen smiled with a lopsided grin. "I'll give you a shout when it's ready if you need some time to put yourselves together."

"Okay," I said. "See you in a few minutes."

After Stephen shut the door behind him, I peered over at Gabby, pinching my eyebrows.

"That was bit *harsh*, don't you think?"

"You don't think he deserved it, after what he said at the beach?"

"Well maybe, but he *did* apologize and sounded like he was genuinely trying to mend bridges..."

"Possibly," she said. "But this has been going on for a long time and I wanted him to realize that I'm not just going to lay over that easily. He's going to have to *earn* my respect to get me back into his good graces."

"And the matrimonial *bed*?"

"That could take a little longer," she said, rubbing her knee softly against my bare thigh. "After last night's experience, I'm in no hurry to rush back into his arms."

"You can't sleep with me *every* night. This girls' sleepover thing will only take us so far."

"True, but he's a pretty sound sleeper, remember? All we have to do is wait until he nods off then I can sneak back into your room. Besides, I'm not finished with you, yet. There's so many more things I want to try before you have to leave..."

"What's the plan for today?" I said, getting up to put on some pants. "It's Sunday. Surely there's *something* we can think of to entice Stephen out of the house for an entire day to take his mind off work."

"I was thinking we could make a trip out to Key West. It's a beautiful drive over the causeway, and there's so much to do there. Quaint shops, great restaurants, and tons of bars to kick up our heels again if you're up for it."

"Oh I'm up for it, alright," I smiled. "But I think it would be better for you and your *husband* to do a little bumping and grinding instead to begin repairing your frosty marriage."

"Maybe," she said. "But first we need to entice him out of the house and away from his computer. We might need to drag him kicking and screaming."

"If that's what it takes," I chuckled. "I'm determined to get you two reconnected if it's the last thing I do."

"Oh?" she teased, stroking the inside of my thigh softly. "You're ready to ditch me this fast? Have your way with me, then dispose of me like so much flotsam?"

"Don't be silly," I said, leaning in toward her and giving her a long, wet kiss. "You know how I feel about you. It's just like you said last night, we can't stay together this way when this week is over. But I'm always going to have a soft spot for you in my heart, no matter where we find ourselves."

"I hope that's not the *only* soft spot you keep reserved for me," she purred, rolling her hand over the front of my panties and stroking my vulva.

"You know it, girl," I smiled. "Whenever we have a chance to reconnect, I'm ready for more fireworks."

"And *car washes*?" she said, raising a playful eyebrow.

"Absolutely, you can hose down my chassis any time you like."

I reached down behind her back and slapped her butt playfully.

"Now get out there and spend some time with your handsome husband before he burns himself on the stove or cuts himself slicing the onions. The last thing we need is for him to have another excuse not to go out with us today."

***

After we got dressed, the three of us had a long relaxing breakfast on the back terrace. The smell of the tropical flowers was intoxicating, and I could feel the fresh sea breeze wafting over from the bay a few miles away. After much begging and pleading, we convinced Stephen to join us on our trip to Key West, where we had a relaxing day exploring the shops and enjoying outdoor dining watching the seabirds trying to steal our scraps. Key West had a large and vibrant LGBT community, and we all had a fun time watching some drag shows and cabaret acts, then dancing at some of the town's hotspots until well after midnight. Stephen and Gabby appeared to be reconnecting as they bumped their bodies together on the dance floor and I even noticed them holding hands while watching some of the shows.

By the long drive home, I was convinced the two of them were ready to climb into bed together to begin rekindling their intimate relationship. But when we stopped to refuel the car at a pitstop along the way, Stephen's mood suddenly became more somber when he got back in the car.

"What is it, hon?" Gabby said, noticing the familiar tightening of his face.

"I just noticed a text message from my boss earlier in the day. He wants me to prepare a presentation for an important meeting first thing tomorrow morning–"

"You've *got* to be kidding me," Gabby groaned, leaning sullenly against the side of her door. "Can't those guys *ever* leave you alone and let you enjoy a full relaxing weekend once in a while?'

"I'm so sorry, Gab," he sighed. "Believe me, this is the last thing I want to be working on tonight. I was really looking forward to having you back in my arms and getting back to the way we were. I promise, after this is done, I'm going to find a way to pull back from this ridiculous work schedule. Jade's visit has really helped me realize the important things I've been neglecting these past few years."

Gabby uttered a heavy sigh and crossed her arms, staring out the side of the window at the wide expanse of the Atlantic Ocean on the side of the Overseas Highway. I could feel the tension in the car, but decided it was best for me to stay out of their domestic troubles for the time being. If Stephen was genuine about his intentions, at least they'd have a fighting chance to repair their fragile marriage at another time.

When we got home, Stephen went to his study to begin work on his presentation, and Gabby insisted on joining me again in my bedroom even though her husband would be awake for another couple of hours. She told him that she was going to spend the night with me again and not to disturb us since we were exhausted after spending two nights in a row without much sleep. He nodded grudgingly, and Gabby shut the door of the den behind her when she left him to his work.

"Are you sure you should be sleeping here again tonight?" I said when she joined me in my bedroom, closing the door softly behind her.

"His study's on the other side of the house," she said, walking directly up to me and beginning to unbutton my blouse. "There's two closed doors between us, and he'll be so absorbed in getting ready for his executive meeting tomorrow morning that he'll pay no mind to whatever we're doing in here."

"I don't know, Gab," I said, pulling away a few inches. "You guys looked to be reconnecting tonight, and I don't want to put another roadblock between the two of you getting back together intimately. Maybe you should wait for him to return to bed. It sounded like he was eager to make love to you again..."

"There'll be plenty of time for that after you leave," she said, stepping forward to kiss me hard on my lips. "We've only got a few days together to share some quality time together. Besides, we've got unfinished business from last night–"

"Mmm," I said, beginning to succumb to her gentle caresses and probing of my nether regions. "Maybe just for a few minutes..."

Gabby tore off my clothes and the two of us pounced on the bed together, temporarily leaving our troubles behind. After rolling back and forth, kissing and rubbing our bodies together, Gabby pinned my arms to the mattress and looked me squarely in the eyes.

"It's *my* turn to taste you tonight," she grinned. "I've been dreaming about licking your pussy from the moment you walked into my house three days ago."

"Are you sure you know *how*?" I kidded. "It's not quite the same as going down on a man. Our body parts are configured a little differently you know..."

"Really?" she said. "I had no idea. Maybe I'll just take your lead from last night and copy what you do. You seem to know your way around a girl's body pretty well."

"I've had a bit more practice," I smiled. "But you seem to be picking up the technique pretty fast–"

"Mmm, especially that whole squirting thing. I can't wait to feel you gushing all over my face while I'm planted between your legs."

"Damn, girl," I sighed. "You're not making this any easier for me to resist your temptations."

"Just lie back and enjoy it then," she said, using my line from the previous night. "Because by the time I'm finished with you, I intend to have you squealing like a little girl."

"Yes," I purred. "Suck my cunny, Gab. I want to feel your pretty lips on my pussy and feel me coming in your mouth."

"Your wish is my command," Gabby said, beginning to kiss her way down my body as she nibbled and lapped up my tingling skin.

It didn't take long for her to bring me to the brink of orgasm as she expertly sucked and rubbed every sensitive area of my private parts, culminating with a long and sustained focus on my flaring clit. But when she thrust three fingers into my hole as I was nearing my peak and began to fuck me hard with her hand while she simultaneously sucked on my nub, she quickly put me over the top, and I grabbed her head hard between my legs, shaking and quivering while trying to stifle my moans of pleasure so Stephen wouldn't hear us.

After I came down from my highs, Gabby scurried up next to me and kissed me softly on the lips, smiling at me.

"Are you sure you haven't done that before?" I said, still breathing heavily. "Because that was some pretty first-rate pussy-licking you were doing right there."

"I might have watched a few lesbian porn videos awaiting your arrival," she smirked. "I wanted to be ready just in case I had the chance to divert your attention away from your brother."

"It looks like you've accomplished your goal," I said, tasing my juices on her tongue as I kissed her passionately.

"Maybe not *entirely*," she said, wrinkling her brow at me. "I didn't feel you squirt when you came, like last time. Did I do something wrong?"

"No, of course not," I said, drawing her closer. "It's not something you can just turn on and off. It depends on a lot of things. How wet I am, how long of a buildup I've had, the position I'm in, and other things. But it felt wonderful, believe me. I had a lovely long orgasm and it felt incredible feeling your face between my legs when I came."

"I'll guess I'll have to take your word for it," Gabby frowned. "But I was kind of looking forward to another 'car-wash' experience, like the one we had in the dressing room at Saks. That was incredibly hot!"

"Oh?" I said, looking at her mischievously. "You like grinding our pussies together and feeling me spraying all over you when I come?"

"Fuck yes," Gabby said, rubbing her mound against mine under the covers.

"I've kind of been wanting to do that again *too* since the last time," I said. "But with both of us moving around together on the bed, we're going to have to be extra careful not to distract Stephen from his work. Are you sure you're going to be able to keep relatively quiet if we do this?"

"I promise," Gabby said, holding up three fingers with

the Girl Scout's pledge. "I just want to feel your wet pussy against mine again. Maybe we can experience a little water-works show together this time."

"I like the sound of that," I said. "But let *me* do most of the work so you don't have to move around too much."

"Whatever you say, boss," Gabby smiled. "Have your way with me. I'll be the sub and you can be the domme. Isn't that kind of how it works with lesbians most of the time?"

"Sometimes, I said. "It depends on who's playing the bottom and who's on top, so to speak. But I'll be happy to take charge this time."

I grabbed Gabby's legs and pushed them apart into a scissors position then turned my body around and wedged my hips between hers.

"Now come here little girl while I give you a proper lesbian fucking."

"Mmm," Gabby purred. "Rub your cunt against mine and make me squeal like a little girl. I want to *watch* you this time while you spray all over my bare pussy."

I grabbed Gabby's knees and pulled her hard toward me, and she groaned when our wet pussies touched. As I began to rock my hips in rhythm with hers, I could hear the sloshing sound of our snatches grinding against one another, and she reached out her arms to join hands with me while we looked into each other's eyes as our passion slowly escalated. The closer we came to approaching our climax, the more tightly we pulled on each other's arms while curling our bodies together, until her back was arched over the mattress and I was kneeling over top of her, grinding my cunt into her upturned pussy.

I could see Gabby's mouth progressively widening as she approached her orgasm, trying desperately not to cry out in pleasure with her body consumed in passion. The sight of her prostrated beneath me at the height of ecstasy, with her pretty tits swaying in tandem with our hips and her big nipples pointing up at me, was simply too much for me to hold back any longer. With one last hard grunt, I mashed my pussy hard against hers and began spraying my juices in every direction as the tight connection between us acted like a spigot, drenching her upper torso and face with my pent-up lubrication.

"Oh my God!" Gabby groaned. "I'm going to come, Jade. I'm going to cum so hard against your pussy. *Uhnnnn!*"

Suddenly, we had *two* powerful jets of lubrication spraying out the sides of both of our pussies, soaking our bodies and the bedsheets thoroughly. I barely noticed how much noise the two of us had been making while lost in the throes of one of the longest and most powerful orgasms I'd experienced in a long time. But just as we began to slow the jerking our hips together in the final stages of our mutual orgasm, we heard another loud tap on our door, and we quickly scrambled under the covers.

"Is everything okay in there?" Stephen called out. "I heard some strange sounds and wondered if something happened."

"Everything's fine," I called back. "We were just laughing about that drag show we were watching earlier in the day."

"I'm finally finished preparing my presentation," Stephen said. "Are you coming to bed, Gabby? I really was hoping we could spend the rest of the night together."

Gabby peered over at me, and I nodded.

"You should go now," I whispered. "Go spend some quality time with your husband while you have the chance. Just clean up quickly in the washroom so he doesn't suspect what you've been up to. Go get your groove on, girl."

"I *am* still kind of horny," she said, smiling at me. "Are

you sure you're going to be alright spending the rest of the night alone?"

"Absolutely," I said. "Nothing would give me more pleasure than to hear the sound of you two renewing your intimate relationship." I nudged her in the side and playfully pushed her out of the bed. "Now go scoot and get reacquainted what it feels like to make love to a *man* for a change!"

"I'm coming babe," Gabby called out. "Just give me a minute and I'll be right there. Maybe you could light some candles and put on some sexy music to get me in the mood..."

"I'm way ahead of you girl," he called back. "And Jade, maybe you should put in some earplugs or wear your headphones for the next hour or so. I wouldn't want to interrupt your sleep any more than I've already done."

"Don't you worry about me," I said. "I'll be fine here all by myself. It's about time you two got back together. Just don't break a gasket or something trying to make up for lost time!"

5

After Gabby left my room and joined Stephen in their bedroom, I could hear some muffled voices under the soft music. But after a few minutes, the bed began to squeak and I heard some gentle moans. As the thumping sound began to grow louder and faster, Gabby became more vocal, and I could hear them quite distinctly.

"Yes, Steve," she panted. "Fuck me, baby."

"Uhnn," I heard Stephen groaning, as the bed squeaked more forcefully.

Even with the sound of soft music playing in the background, I could make out almost everything they were saying, and I wondered if Stephen had also heard Gabby and me making love earlier in the night. *Had hearing her enjoying herself while having sex with me been the cause of his renewed interest in his wife?* I knew most guys were obsessed with the idea of two girls getting it on, or even better, a three-way *menage*, but getting turned on with his sister in the mix seemed kind of creepy.

Nevertheless, the more noise they made from the other room, the more excited I became listening to them. I could still feel Gabby's juices dripping down over my tits and stomach, and while I listened to them making love in the adjacent bedroom, I threaded my hand down between my legs and began to play with my clit.

"*God*, Gabby," Stephen panted. "You feel so good. We have *got* to do this more often."

"I hope so," Gabby said. "You don't want me looking for *other* outlets for my sexual needs, do you?"

"It depends what those outlets are," Stephen said. "You know how much I used to love watching you play with your vibrators."

"Yeah, well, sometimes a girl needs to feel some real flesh and juices once in a while."

"I'll be giving you some of *my* juice pretty soon," Stephen grunted, renewing his pace.

"Hold up for a sec," Gabby said, and suddenly everything stopped in the other room. "I want to feel you come in me from *behind*."

I heard the sound of the bed squeaking and the rustling of sheets, then Stephen groaned when he slid his cock back into Gabby's pussy in the doggy-style position.

"*That's* the way I like it," Gabby hissed. "Pound my ass with your big meat, Steve."

"Jesus, Gab," he panted. "We haven't done it this way since our college days. What's come over you?"

"Quite a bit, actually," she teased. "Let's just say I've gotten a new appreciation for adding a little variety to my sex life."

"Whatever the reason, I *like* it," Stephen said, beginning to breathe more heavily as the headboard pounded harder against the wall.

"Yes, Steve," Gabby panted. "Pound my ass harder. Slap your balls against my wet pussy."

"Yeah, baby," he said. "Talk dirty to me. We haven't had sex like this in ages."

"There's a lot more of this waiting for you if you can drag yourself away from work more often. Lean over and squeeze my tits. I want to feel your hot breath on my neck when you come inside me."

"Fuck, yeah," Steve grunted, shifting his weight forward. "You know I love your tits. Your nipples feel so firm."

"Pinch them, baby," Gabby growled. "Squeeze me harder. I'm going to come all over your big dick soon."

"Here it comes, baby," he said. "Oh God–I'm coming!!"

"*Ngah!*" Gabby suddenly groaned with a loud sloshing sound.

"What the–" Stephen said. "Holy fuck! *Unghhhh!!*"

I heard both of them moaning for many long seconds as it became apparent that Gabby was showing off her newfound squirting skills with her husband, and Stephen was undeniably enjoying the sensation of her spraying all over his balls while he rammed her from behind. The image in my head of my two favorite people in the world climaxing together in a mutual shower of cum made me overjoyed, and I rammed my fingers into my pussy, soon after reaching my own climax.

Seconds later, I rolled over and flitted my eyes shut, feeling the effects of the late nights catching up with me as I began to nod off.

It looks like my work is done here, I smiled contentedly.

R*eady for more erotic chills and thrills? Choose your next toe-curling fantasy from over thirty-five spicy stories in Jade's Erotic Adventures. Browse the full collection here:*

Click to scan your favorites...

FOLLOW VICTORIA RUSH:

Want to keep informed of my latest erotic book releases? Sign up for my newsletter and receive a FREE bonus book:

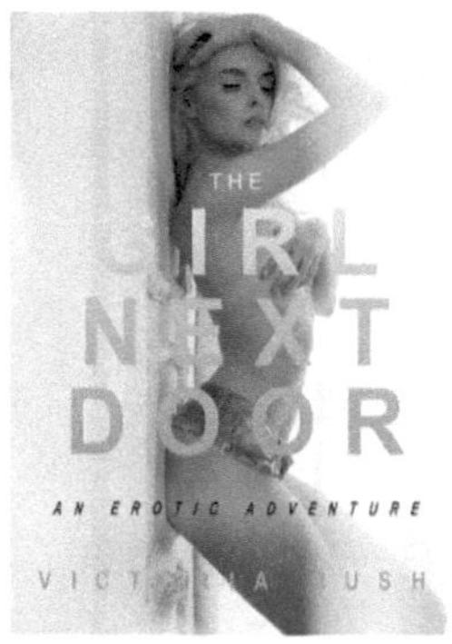

Spying on the neighbors just got a lot more interesting...

9 781990 118517